Jumbo Jets

My Mum

Dee Shulman

Look out for more *Jumbo Jets* from Collins

Finlay MacTrebble and the Fantastic Fertiliser • **Scoular Anderson**

Forecast of Fear • **Keith Brumpton**

Trouble on the Day • **Norma Clarke**

The Curse of Brian's Brick • **James Andrew Hall**

Invasion of the Dinner Ladies • *Pickles Sniffs it Out* • **Michaela Morgan**

We Won the Lottery • **Shoo Rayner**

Bernie Works a Miracle • **Leon Rosselson**

Charlie and Biff • *Fergus the Forgetful* • *Fidgety Felix* • *Queen Lizzie Rules OK* • **Margaret Ryan**

The Man in Shades • *Talking Pictures* • **Pat Thomson**

Sir Quinton Quest Hunts the Yeti • *Sir Quinton Quest Hunts the Jewel* • **Kay Umansky**

Gosh Look Teddy, it's a Werewolf • **Bob Wilson**

The Baked Bean Cure • *Dad's Dodgy Lodger* • **Philip Wooderson**

For Flora and Esther

First published by A & C Black Ltd in 1996
Published by Collins in 1997
10 9 8 7 6 5 4 3
Collins is an imprint of HarperCollins*Publishers* Ltd,
77–85 Fulham Palace Road, Hammersmith, London W6 8JB

ISBN 0 00 675284-5

Text © 1996 Dee Shulman

The author asserts the moral right to be identified as the author of the work.
A CIP record for this title is available from the British Library.
Printed and bound in Great Britain by
Bookmarque Ltd, Croydon, Surrey

CHAPTER ONE
Meet Mum

Imagine this.

It's your first day in a new school.

You're standing next to your mum, in a line with a load of other kids. And you don't know any of them. You're trying to put a brave face on it. Trying not to do or say anything that will make anyone look at you.

Then the teacher comes along to take you into your classroom. You say 'Goodbye' to your mum, pick up your P.E. bag and follow the others as casually as you can.

Just when you think it's all gone smoothly, this huge singing voice suddenly echoes around the building . . .

Bye-bye Rosie-Pooh...SOB... My baby in top juniors...How can I bear it? ...SOB...

Rosie, just one more kiss... SOB...

...I'm missing you already...

And as you stand there, transfixed with horror, you realise that everyone is looking at this wailing woman in the fake-fur coat. And as the hot redness spreads from your neck to your ears, you watch her running towards you . . .

You have a nano-second to decide whether you can make it through the Fire Exit before she gets to you.

But you dither a moment too long and she is there, enveloping you in blackness and wet tears.

Ha!

snigger

chortle

!

When you finally emerge, coughing and breathless, you're surrounded by a class of staring, sniggering children, and a dumbstruck teacher.

Tee Hee!

Hee! Hee!

Ha

Just when you think it's all over, your mum looks at you once more.

You close your eyes.

You know.

You have two red lips glowing on your cheeks.

And while your thoughts are swimming around in the nightmare of the situation, the nightmare gets worse.

Your mum has found an old tissue in her pocket. She is spitting on it, and now . . . she is cleaning your face with it!

In front of everyone . . .

CHAPTER TWO
Mum's morning off

Luckily, for the first couple of weeks at my new school, Mum was really busy. She's an actress, and the play she was acting in was about to open, so she virtually lived at the theatre.

This meant that our au pair, Helga, had to take me to and from school. Helga is quiet, and speaks hardly any English. Ideal.

Ja, good, okay!

The kids in my class were just beginning to get bored with calling me 'Rosie-Pooh' and blowing me loud wet kisses, when disaster struck . . . Mum had a morning off.

GULP!

I climbed forlornly into the back of the car.

Well?

said Mum, in the kind of voice she'd use to fill a Roman amphitheatre.

Lead me to your beautiful pictures, ♪ your wonderful stories, your ♪ incredible maths...

As I feared, the classroom was full.

Oh here are all your little ♪ chums! How enchanting!

The 'little chums' were totally silent.

But I don't see your teacher, Rosie. Is this usual? No wonder your work isn't on the wall if she's never here—

Good morning class—

interrupted Miss Block.

I squeaked desperately.

'After school next Thursday would be a good time to discuss your daughter's progress,' said Miss Block, steering Mum towards the door. 'Shall we say 4 o'clock?'

She had got Mum out of the room! I breathed a sigh of relief.

Big mistake.

She was back!

I shut my eyes. Perhaps I could will myself into another life, another world. Narnia would be nice . . .

But Miss Block came to the rescue.

And she firmly shut the door.

11

CHAPTER FOUR
The tea

Mum was still on at me about having someone to tea three days later.

If I didn't invite someone soon, she was threatening to do it for me.

I decided to ask Amy Burton.
She had only been my
dinner-partner twice, but
she had let me join in the
skipping at lunchtime,
and hadn't called me
'Rosie-petal' once.

But I had to plan it cunningly.

I carefully consulted the calendar on the
fridge, to check when Mum would definitely
be rehearsing late at the theatre . . .

. . . and invited Amy on the 23rd.

Because we don't have any normal food in the house,

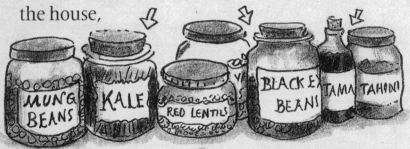

I spent the whole week going through menus with Helga and a dictionary.

We decided to buy the food on the way home from school. That way, Mum wouldn't find anything suspicious in the fridge.

Everything was going as planned. At 3.30 pm on the 23rd, Helga came to meet Amy and me from school, and we stopped off at the shops to buy . . .

So far so good.

Helga had just yelled,

Ja, eet's READY!

when a terrible sound echoed through the house.

It was the rattle of my mother's key in the lock!

Helga and I exchanged looks of total panic. Amy just looked puzzled.

COOEEE darlings! I'm home ♫ EARLEEE! Isn't it WONDER—

Mum never finished that sentence. She came into the room with her face wrinkled into an horrific expression.

What is that FOUL smell? Has 'Burger Box' moved next door? GOOD LORD!

WHAT'S THAT?

What could I do?

Phone the NSPCC?

Lead Amy and Helga out through the front door, never to return again?

Or stare miserably down at the floor, and wish I had somebody else's mother?

After careful consideration, I chose the third option.

But Mum's attention wasn't on *me* . . .

And she began assembling:

I suppose, looking on the bright side, there were two good things about that evening.

 The first was that when Mum cooks she sings. This in itself is obviously not good. It is deeply painful. But, when she is singing, she can't be talking, so Amy and I got to watch the whole episode of *Our Street* on telly in peace.

20

The second good thing was that Amy never actually had to eat Mum's creation, because her dad came to collect her long before it was cooked.

Going home starving was, believe me, a lucky break.

CHAPTER FIVE
The trip

I was dreading going into school the next morning. What would Amy tell everyone about the nightmare tea event? Could I get there in time to gag her?

No such luck. Mum's car ran out of petrol, so I was late.

I crept into the classroom, waiting for the whispers and sniggers, but no-one even noticed me. They were all far too interested in what Miss Block was saying.

I'm mad about animals. Dogs, sheep, tarantulas – I love them all.

So the thought of this trip made me forget my worries about the ghastly tea. Miraculously, Amy seemed to have forgotten about it too.

I wandered around dreaming of being the city farm vet, moving from one cured animal to the next.

I couldn't wait!

CHAPTER SIX
The form

When I got home I carefully read
the form Mum had to sign.

Mum wasn't due back till late, so I left the
form on the kitchen table with a pen and a
note next to it.

I went to bed praying that she would say yes.

Next morning, I rushed downstairs . . .

The form was still unsigned, and there was no neat little pile of coins next to it as I had hoped.

I picked up the form and the pen, and ran upstairs again. Mum's door was shut. That meant she was still asleep.

This was the best time.

Very quietly, I crept into her room and carefully picked my way across to her bed.

I tried again.

That must have done the trick!

YES! Operation City Farm was off the ground!

Friday – just the weekend to go.
Surely nothing could go wrong now?

Oh Yes it could!

My mum chose that afternoon, of all the 365
afternoons at her disposal, to come and collect
me from school.

Well, it could have been all right I suppose.
She could have stood quietly by the door,
like all the other parents, and waited
till Miss Block called my name.
Then we could
have walked
home together,
happily planning
our weekend,
maybe stopping
at the sweet shop
for an ice-lolly.

It could have happened like that, but it didn't.

Of course, I *heard* my mother before I saw her.

Can anyone remind me where my daughter Rosie's class is?

-Of course I can't remember her teacher's name! No wait... It's coming to me... Something like **Lump. Frump?**... No- **Clot?**... That's nearer... Ah... **Blot**...

Blot, unfortunately, was close enough. As I looked through the cracks between my sweaty fingers, her apparition filled the doorway.

The only solution was a quick getaway. I put up my hand.

Miss Block, my mum's here - can I go please?

But Miss Block wasn't finished yet. She had to remind the class about the trip. As if we had been talking about anything else all week!

Suddenly she turned to the parents in the doorway and said,

We do still need one more parent to accompany us on this wonderful visit to the Farm and Ecological Centre.

If Miss Block hadn't mentioned 'ecological', Mum would have paid no attention. But 'ecological' is one of Mum's favourite words. I knew she'd hear that.

Ecological Centre! But how marvellous. I knew nothing of this... ...I signed a form?... Really?..when is it? Monday... Let me see...

Oh PLEASE . . . NO! Mum was looking in her diary! It wasn't possible. After all my careful planning . . .

And she started to SING!

CHAPTER EIGHT
Despair

Scientists say that in times of extreme emergency, the body can perform amazing feats of speed and strength.

It's true.

I got Mum out of that building so fast, she didn't even manage to finish the first line of the song.

Back home, I went upstairs to my bedroom.

I think I can genuinely say that I now knew the meaning of true despair.

MY MUM WAS COMING ON THE TRIP!

What could I do? I sat up and wrote out my
options:

1. Get sick
2. Go in disguise
3. Get Mum out of the country

I crossed out the first option straight away.
I was too desperate to go on the trip.

I toyed longer with
the second option . . .

. . . but I wasn't entirely convinced.

That only left the third choice:

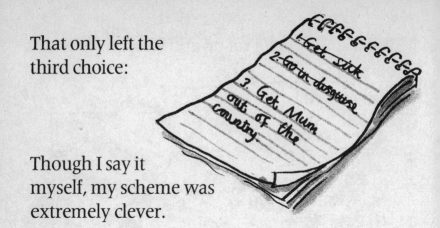

Though I say it myself, my scheme was extremely clever.

After spending ages practising my American accent . . .

. . . I was finally ready. I dialled the theatre.
They went and found her. This was it . . .

I thought it had gone quite well.

It hadn't.

Back to the drawing board.

CHAPTER NINE
Plans

By Monday morning I was down to my last idea.

I woke up early, and crept on to the landing. Mum's door was shut. All I had to do was creep into her room, get her clock, and put the time back a couple of hours. She would oversleep and . . . miss the coach!

I opened the door and tiptoed over to her bed. There was the clock. I leaned over Mum and picked it up.

Now, that clock is not heavy, or slippery.
So why did I have to drop it . . .

Oops!

YEOWW!

CLUNK!

. . . on my mother's head?

WHAT THE — ROSIE...

... what are you doing with my clock?

I stood there guiltily, trying to come up with
an answer.

Then she threw out her arms and kissed me.

And with that, she jumped out of bed.

I hurried back to my room, threw on my clothes . . .

. . . and bolted downstairs to make my packed lunch before Mum could get involved. Of course I knew I'd be the only one without crisps, or a chocolate biscuit, but I wanted to try to avoid her sticking any alfalfa seeds or live yoghurt in my sandwiches.

I had just closed my lunch-box when Mum appeared.

MUM! Where did you get those clothes?

From the theatre wardrobe darling- Aren't they just Perfect?

And she waded into the kitchen.

The excited chatter changed to a giggling silence when Mum entered the classroom. I hung around by the door, so I didn't have to see their faces. This meant that when Robbie Gregson passed me, shouting,

The coach is here!

I was the first in the queue.

I jumped on and managed to get a seat at the back (knowing Mum only sits at the front). When Amy climbed in, I waved frantically to her. She had promised to be my partner, but she acted as if she hadn't seen me. She stopped halfway up the coach, and sat down next to Kunal.

As if this wasn't bad enough, all through the journey I could hear Mum's resounding laugh wafting up from the front.

HA-HA-HA = HA = HA = HA = HA = HA HA

She and Miss Block sounded as though they were having a terrific time.

I looked out of the window, wondering whether I had been swapped at birth. Somewhere, my true family would suddenly realise that they had the wrong child . . .

. . . and come and find me. I was just imagining our joyful reunion, when the coach stopped. We had arrived!

As we piled out of the coach, I looked round cautiously for Mum.

She was in the middle of the road gazing across the fence to the building next door.

How extraordinary! —

she was saying, to no-one in particular.

— That's the TV Studio where we filmed "Abide with Me."

I never noticed this centre, then!

Miss Block, who was busy counting us, told
her that the centre had only just opened, and
told *us* that she expected it to still look clean
and new when we left.

First we saw some tiny piglets all climbing on to this enormous sow.

I was just thinking how sweet they looked, when Mum said,

What **darling** little piggies— Such a shame theyll be bacon sandwiches in a month or two!

Mr Lovegreen gave Mum a very hard stare.

We moved on to the cowshed. Everyone was 'ooohing' and 'aahhhing' at the little calves being fed milk with a baby's bottle, when Mum's echoing voice rang out,

Poor mite-taken away from its mother at birth so she can make plenty of milk for us!

Mr Lovegreen coughed angrily.

asked Miss Block quickly.

The sheep were grazing outside.

My heart sank.

♪ What darling...
DARLING... DARLING...

Was she ill? Had her voice stuck?
Was she having a breakdown?
Oh, PLEASE, not in front of the
whole class!

But Mum wasn't looking at the sheep at all.
Her eyes were fixed on a man on the other
side of the fence. She was waving at him
wildly.

He had heard her.
He had seen her.
He was running towards
the fence. So was she.

Could it get any worse?

51

Yes it could . . . they started . . . hugging each other.

We all rushed to the fence.

My mum turned to us and said,

I tried not to die of shock.
Then Amy came up behind me, and said,

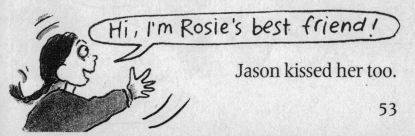

Jason kissed her too.

Then he said,

How would you all like me to get hold of some tickets for the show?

For "OUR STREET"?

TICKETS?

Brilliant!

FANTASTIC!

Wicked!

Okay, it's a deal!

I'll get them sent to Rosie's Mum —

— and she can pass them on to you!

> Now, I must get going or I'll be late. Wonderful to see you again darling!

He gave Mum
another big hug.
Then he waved to us all, and ran off.

The rest of the day passed in a dream.
Everyone hung around me and Mum, asking
what other famous stars we knew.

> Can you get me Michael Jackson's autograph?

> How about Kermit The Frog?

> D'yer know Gazza?

Then before we got on the coach, Amy
grabbed my arm and made me promise to sit
next to her!

CHAPTER TWELVE
Friends

When I woke up next morning, I was filled with a warm glow of pleasure.

Then I panicked. Had it all been a dream? I tried to remember the details:

Jason O'Swoony! . . . . . . my mum – the class celebrity! . . .

. . . and the promise of tickets . . .

. . . to *Our Street*!

But when I got to school, I knew I hadn't been dreaming.

Amy came bounding up to me,

She pulled me into the classroom, and all the
kids came rushing over.

She wasn't, and for the first time in my life I
felt a little twinge of regret.

A few days later Mum did come to collect me. She arrived at the doorway in fluorescent pink and orange.

> Darlings, I've got them — they're here... THE TICKETS!

> Rosie sweetheart, can you give them out?

I was expecting that cringey, please-don't-connect-yourself-with-me-Mum feeling, but instead I was surprised by a totally unfamiliar sensation . . . was it . . . it couldn't be . . . not . . . pride?

I handed round the tickets.

Only two weeks to wait.

Over the next fortnight, I began to realise what it's like to be a star.

Everyone in the class wanted my opinion on last night's TV programmes.

Most of them tried to find some reason or other to drop round to my house, no matter what time . . .

. . . and I got invited to so many teas, I had to make a list.

By the time The Day arrived, I had nearly had enough.
When Mum, Helga and I arrived at the studio, Amy, Gemma and Laura were already there. I had been consulted hundreds of times about what they should wear, but not in my wildest dreams was I prepared for this:

Good Lord!

Miniatures of ME!

Do I really look that funny?

I made no comment.

As she led us to our seats, Mum told us how the sets looked like real rooms, but were really just flat boards, with bits and pieces tacked on.

Once—when I was filming—I leaned against the wall, and it fell over—revealing three technicians drinking tea!...

...The audience screamed with laughter!

So did my class!

HA!

HA!

Oooh please!

Oh tell us another story!

Hee!Hee!

It's about to start...

Mum whispered as quietly as Mum could,

I'll tell you some more later.

We wriggled happily in our seats.

Just as the lights were coming up on the stage, one of the kids chirped out,

ROSIE'S MUM IS THE BEST!

And everyone chorused,

YE-E-E-S!

YE-E-E-S!

YE-E-E-ES!

. . . . including me!

Yesterday, I brought home a note about the school jumble sale.

When I asked Mum if we had any jumble, she staggered downstairs with two suitcases full.

She grinned . . .

The only word that sprang instantly to mind was . . .